THE HARDY BOYS®

SECRET FILES #19

★★ The Race Is On ★★

BY FRANKLIN W. DIXON

ILLUSTRATED BY SCOTT BURROUGHS

ALADDIN · NEW YORK LONDON TORONTO SYDNEY NEW DELHI

ALADDIN

An imprint of Simon & Schuster Children's Publishing Division

1230 Avenue of the Americas, New York, NY 10020

First Aladdin paperback edition December 2015

Text copyright © 2015 by Simon & Schuster, Inc.

Illustrations copyright © 2015 by Scott Burroughs

All rights reserved, including the right of reproduction in whole or in part in any form.

ALADDIN is a trademark of Simon & Schuster, Inc., and related logo is a registered trademark of Simon & Schuster, Inc.

THE HARDY BOYS is a registered trademark of Simon & Schuster, Inc.

For information about special discounts for bulk purchases, please contact Simon & Schuster Special Sales at 1-866-506-1949 or business@simonandschuster.com.

The Simon & Schuster Speakers Bureau can bring authors to your live event. For more information or to book an event contact the Simon & Schuster Speakers Bureau at 1-866-248-3049 or visit our website at www.simonspeakers.com.

Series design by Lisa Vega

Cover design by Karina Granda

The text of this book was set in Garamond.

Manufactured in the United States of America 1015 OFF

10 9 8 7 6 5 4 3 2 1

Library of Congress Control Number 2014957740

ISBN 978-1-4814-2271-0 (pbk)

ISBN 978-1-4814-2272-7 (eBook)

⋆⋆ CONTENTS ⋆⋆

Bet on Chet!

"Chet Morton for class president!" Frank called out. He shoved buttons into Lizzy Kahn's and Elisa Hernandez's hands as they walked past. He and Joe had made a hundred of the buttons last week for their friend Chet Morton. Each one said BET ON CHET! in giant blue letters.

Joe stood beside Chet as he greeted all the Bayport Elementary students that came through the front doors of the school. It was just before the first bell. Everyone was in their fall clothes—

brand-new jeans, and T-shirts from different places where they'd vacationed over the summer.

"I hope you'll vote for me tomorrow," Chet said to Matilda Goodwin, a girl from his class. She was wearing a Disneyland shirt. "Bayport Elementary is ready for a change!"

"Take a cookie," Joe whispered to Matilda, pointing to the table in front of them. Mrs. Hardy had sent them to school with a batch of her famous double chocolate chip cookies. It helped bring people over to their side of the lobby.

"Do you really think I have a chance?" Chet whispered, glancing across the lobby. Cissy Zermeño was standing there with their other friend Phil Cohen. Behind them was a whole row of posters. TRUST IN CISSY, RE-ELECT CISSY ZERMEÑO, and YOU THINK SHE'S SO NICE, VOTE FOR HER TWICE! Cissy had been president for one year already, and most of the class really liked her. Frank, Joe, and Chet liked her too—she was one of their friends, and she played with them on their baseball team, the Bayport Bandits.

"Of course you have a chance," Frank said. "We wouldn't be your campaign managers if we didn't think you had a chance."

"Cissy's great, but it's time to give someone else a try. Our class needs a change," Joe added. "Who's better to do that than you?"

Chet greeted a few more students as they walked in the door, shaking hands with them like a real politician. He was wearing a collared shirt and khakis. He'd worn almost the same outfit every day for two weeks, since the campaign had started. "I guess I'm just nervous," he said after a group from their gym class left.

"It's normal to be nervous," Joe said. He was eight years old and the younger of the two Hardy brothers, with blond hair and blue eyes. His older brother, nine-year-old Frank, had dark brown hair and brown eyes, and looked much more like their dad, Fenton. Fenton Hardy was a private investigator in Bayport. The boys had learned everything they knew about solving mysteries from him.

Frank grabbed a poster from beside the table, unrolled it, and taped it to the wall. It said CHANGE YOU CAN TRUST: CHET MORTON FOR CLASS PRESIDENT in bubble letters. "Maybe you should practice the speech again," Frank said. "It's pretty awesome."

Joe looked around the school lobby. Most of the kids had gone inside their classrooms already.

Even Phil and Cissy were packing up their table. "Let's just wait until they go . . . ," Joe whispered. He wasn't usually so suspicious of people, but everyone was saying it was going to be a close vote tomorrow. Many students had promised to vote for Chet, but promises didn't mean they would actually do what they'd said. It was going to come down to the speeches. They couldn't let Cissy know what he planned to say.

When Phil had put all the CISSY FOR PRES buttons and pens back in their shoebox, the two of them came over to Chet's table. "Good luck tomorrow," Cissy said, reaching out her hand. "May the best candidate win."

Frank glanced sideways at his brother. Cissy was the pitcher for the Bandits, and it seemed like she was always winning at everything! But even though she'd won the talent show last year and the science fair the year before that, it was hard not to like her. She was always so nice and always did the right thing.

"You too," Chet said, shaking Cissy's hand. Phil stood beside her, and for the first time Frank noticed that the button he wore lit up. CISSY'S #1! it said, the number one glowing white. Frank could tell Phil had made it himself—he was always making little gadgets. He loved playing with robots or taking apart his parents' old computers.

"We'll see you tomorrow at the assembly," Phil said, before the two of them turned to go.

When they had disappeared down the hall, Chet pulled the folded speech from his pocket. The paper was worn in places because he'd practiced the speech so much. "Ready?" he asked, looking from Frank to Joe.

"You bet," Joe said.

Chet cleared his throat and began. "Good morning, students of Bayport Elementary. Most of you know me already, but my name is Chet Morton and I'm running for fourth-grade class president." Chet looked up at his friends, trying to see if he'd read the first lines well enough. "What do you think? I want to sound friendly but not too friendly."

"It's perfect!" Frank encouraged. "Keep going!"

Chet grinned and continued. "We can all agree this is a great place to go to school, but I think some things around here can be better. If you elect me class president, the first thing I'll do is talk to all of you and hear about what you want to change."

A few girls came in from outside, talking about a school dance that was being held next week. Chet stopped until they'd passed. When he began again, he talked about all the things he wanted to do for their class. He would get them better lunch choices in the school cafeteria and get picnic benches so they could eat lunch outside if they wanted to. He had another idea called "New Voices." He wanted to give different students a chance to read the morning announcements, instead of having the same people do it every time. Joe's and Frank's favorite idea was for a School Sports Night, where teachers and students would compete for prizes.

"If you give me a chance to be your president," Chet continued, "I'll do my best to listen to your ideas and make them happen. And more than anything, I want our class to be closer than ever. Together we can make a change."

Chet looked up from his paper, waiting to see Frank's and Joe's reactions. Both of the boys cheered and clapped.

"Every word was perfect," Frank said.

"Who wouldn't vote for you?" Joe asked.

As the bell rang to start class, Frank and Joe collected the BET ON CHET! buttons and their chocolate chip cookies. They ate the last of them while they walked Chet to class.

"Now we just have to wait for tomorrow," Chet said, folding the speech into his pocket. "I'll try not to get too nervous. But every time I think of it, it's hard. More than a hundred students, all in the gym . . ."

"You're going to be great," Frank said, giving Chet a high-five. "You have nothing to worry about."

"You sure?" Chet asked. He pushed his hands deep into his pockets, the way he always did when he was nervous. "I don't know anymore."

Joe glanced at his brother, then back at their friend. He put another one of the BET ON CHET! buttons on the front of his shirt, where everyone could see. "I'm positive," Joe said. "Tomorrow you're going to rock!"

To Chet, that just meant a lot more kids listening, and he was super nervous.

Joe went to the gym doors and pointed inside. "Look at all the people who are waiting to hear you talk," he said. "Look how many people are wearing buttons and holding signs."

He waved for Chet to come up behind him and see. All three boys stood in the doorway, looking in. They could see two of their friends, Callie and Ellie, holding up signs near the back that said CHET MORTON FOR PRESIDENT. Half of the front row was wearing BET ON CHET! buttons, including a bunch of kids from Chet's classes.

Chet smiled at the group of friends in the second row chanting, "CHET! CHET! CHET!"

"Everyone is rooting for you," Frank said, handing Chet his speech. He gave him a pat on the back. "You can do this."

Chet took a deep breath as the crowd in the gym

finally went quiet. Art Carson, one of the shortest kids in the fourth-grade class, came to the microphone. He had glasses and spiky black hair. He emceed nearly every event at Bayport Elementary and took his job very seriously. "Good morning, Bayport students!" he yelled in his signature whiny voice. He sounded a little like a squeaky hinge. "Today you'll be hearing from two candidates for fourth-grade class president—your current president Cissy Zermeño, and her big competition, Chet Morton!"

Art glanced into the doorway, making sure Chet was there. Frank and Joe stood right behind him. Even though Joe wasn't in Chet and Frank's grade, he gave himself the title of honorary campaign manager. Since Frank was helping his friend "officially" they were both able to stay with him before the speech. He was up first, then Cissy.

Frank looked down at the paper in Chet's hands. He realized Chet was shaking. "You're going to be great," Frank reminded him. "Read it just like you practiced."

Chet wiped the sweat off his forehead with one hand, then adjusted his clip-on tie. "Right," he repeated. "Just like I practiced."

"First up is Chet Morton," Art continued up onstage. "You've seen him playing for the Bayport Bandits or working at the wood shop after school. But lately he's been in the school lobby every morning with chocolate chip cookies, telling you why you should vote for him." Art put his hand out, pointing to the door. "Let's give it up for Chet Morton!"

Chet turned back to Frank and Joe and smiled one last time before walking to the stage. He waved to Callie and Ellie in the back row as he passed. Frank could tell he was more nervous than ever. His whole face was red, and he took twice as long as normal to climb the three stairs to the platform. He was obviously worried he was going to trip.

When he finally got to the microphone, he cleared his throat and looked out into the crowd. Everyone was quiet. Dr. Green sat in the front row, smiling up at Chet. "Good morning, students of Bayport Elementary. Most of you know me already, but my name is Chet Morton and I'm running for fourth-grade class president."

A group of boys in the back of the gym let out a few loud hoots. "Go, Chet!" one of them yelled. Joe squinted, trying to make out who it was. It looked like Jason Prime, the first baseman for the Bandits.

Chet laughed into the microphone. "We can all agree this is—"

Suddenly Chet was cut off as a sheet of green slime rained down from the ceiling. It dripped onto his hair, over his face, and down the front of his shirt. Frank and Joe stood in the doorway, shocked.

"What is that?" Frank asked.

They both looked up to the ceiling, where a

small blue bucket was sitting on one of the rafters, with almost half the bucket off the edge. It was upright, but the green slime was dribbling down from a small trapdoor that flapped open at the bottom. Chet stood there underneath it, looking dazed. He was still holding his speech, which was soaked.

The kids started laughing. "Someone slimed him!" a boy in the back yelled out.

Dr. Green stood up, waving for the boy to be quiet. "Enough! Who did this? Who wants to tell me what's going on?"

Chet wiped the slime from his eyes. He shook it from his hands. Frank and Joe had never seen their friend more upset. His bottom lip was shaking. When he glanced over at them, he looked like he might cry at any moment.

Then he ran down the stage steps and disappeared into the hall.

 **3**

A Sticky Situation

Everyone, quiet down!" Dr. Green yelled. "Who is responsible for this?"

The kids in the front row stopped laughing. They looked around, waiting for someone to say something. Nobody did.

"Who would do that?" Frank asked, turning to his brother. "It's so . . . mean."

"I don't know, but we need to find Chet," Joe said. The boys slipped out of the gym and into the main lobby. They could still hear Dr. Green yelling. She said something about pranks not being allowed at Bayport, and that whoever did this would be punished.

Frank and Joe went toward the boys' bathroom first. It looked completely empty.

"Chet?" Frank glanced around. Chet wasn't at the sinks. Frank turned to the stalls,

looking down the row. "Chet, it's us. Frank and Joe. Are you there?"

"They embarrassed me!" a voice called out from the last stall. "I can't go back out there."

Frank walked down to the last bathroom stall and opened it. Chet was there, a wad of toilet paper in his hands. He wiped some of the green slime from the front of his shirt, but it was still all over him—in his hair, on his face. It was even caught in his eyebrows.

"I'm sorry this happened to you," Joe said. He hated seeing his friend like this. He grabbed another ball of toilet paper and handed it to Chet. "Whoever did it was trying to ruin your campaign. They must've been afraid you were going to win."

"We don't know what happened," Frank said. He didn't want to jump to any conclusions. "But it seems like it was meant to wreck your big moment onstage. Come on," he said, waving Chet out of the stall. "Let's get you cleaned up."

They walked Chet over to the sinks and turned on the water. Chet leaned down and rinsed his face. He took the slippery pink soap from the dispenser nearby and washed his arms and his face, trying to get the gross goo from behind his ears. When he was done, Joe handed him some paper towels.

"I can't go back out there—not now, not ever," Chet said, wiping his eyes. "It was so embarrassing. Everyone was laughing at me."

"Everyone loves you, Chet," Frank said. "They were just laughing because . . . I don't know, because they think slime is funny? It didn't mean anything."

"They think I'm a joke. How am I supposed to be class president when I just got slimed in front of everyone? No one's going to vote for me now." Chet slumped his shoulders.

"That's not true!" Joe said.

"I can't go back onto that stage," Chet repeated. "I won't."

Just then there was a knock on the door. "Chet? Can you come out here so I can talk to you?"

Frank and Joe recognized Dr. Green's voice. Chet looked at them, then shook his head.

"We'll come with you," Joe promised. He walked beside Chet as they went to the door.

When they got there, Dr. Green was standing right outside. Behind her the gymnasium was emptying out. Kids left through the back doors, and some through the doors on the side. No one was laughing or whispering. Everyone seemed serious as they filed out.

"Chet, I'm so glad you're okay," Dr. Green said. She looked at Chet's face, which was mostly clean except for a little smudge of green stuff on his chin. She seemed relieved he wasn't hurt.

"Yeah, I guess." Chet lowered his head. He used the last of the toilet paper to wipe some of the slime from his shirt.

"Well, I'm glad you have good friends to look after you," Dr. Green said, giving Frank and Joe a small smile. "I'm sorry this happened. I've decided to postpone the fourth-grade speeches until tomorrow morning, and we can hold the election tomorrow afternoon."

"I don't think I can give another speech . . . ," Chet said sadly. He glanced in the direction of the auditorium. "Not after that."

"I know it's upsetting," Dr. Green said. "But we're going to find whoever did this. We don't allow pranks, especially not like this. The person will be caught and punished, and tomorrow you'll give your speech without having to worry."

"I don't know about that," Chet said, shaking his head.

Dr. Green didn't seem to hear him. She smiled, her hands clasped together. "Don't worry, Chet. We're going to find out who did this," she repeated. "You can redo your speech, and everyone will vote tomorrow afternoon!"

Chet kept trying to wipe the last bit of slime from his shirt. His clip-on tie was stained, and there was green goo on his new sneakers. "I just hope people will still vote for me," he whispered.

Frank glanced sideways at his brother, knowing that it didn't matter what Dr. Green said. They could put the voting off until tomorrow afternoon. That wasn't the problem. Unless they found out who had put that bucket above the stage, the election wouldn't go on, no matter how much anyone wanted it to. There was no way Chet was going to give another speech unless they found out who had done this.

4

Unusual Suspects

Why don't I write you all a pass for the rest of the afternoon," Dr. Green said, pulling out a notepad. "You're allowed to take some time, Chet. Maybe you can change into some clean clothes? There are some shirts and shorts in the lost and found."

Chet frowned at the mention of the lost and found. Everyone had seen the box in the main office, with old ripped sweatshirts and stray socks. One time there'd been a hat that had said

GO BANANAS! with three monkeys on the front of it. No one had ever come back to claim it.

"I'll just use my gym clothes," Chet said.

Dr. Green turned to Frank and Joe. "Let me know if you need any help with anything, boys," she said, handing them the hall passes. "I'm going to do my own investigating. Hopefully together we'll figure this one out."

"We're on the case," Frank said. He and Joe were known for solving mysteries around Bayport. When the school time capsule had been stolen last year, Frank and Joe had been the ones who'd found it. They'd helped their neighbors and friends find missing watches and jewelry, and they'd even turned up a few lost dogs along the way. Dr. Green often asked for their help when something went wrong.

"Glad to hear it. I'm going to call one of the janitors to clean up the mess." Dr. Green took off to find help, and then turned back to head toward the main office. When she was gone, Joe pulled his notepad from his back pocket and looked at Chet.

"Let's get to work, then," Joe said. He started to scribble *Who, What, When, Where, Why,* and *How* down on the page, as they made their way back to the gym. They always started with those six words when they were investigating a mystery. Their

father had taught them that asking these questions helped them see the case from all different sides. Sometimes it turned up clues they hadn't even realized were there.

"What and Where—those are easy," Frank said. "A sliming in the gymnasium."

"A *sliming*?" Chet said, his eyes wide. "Isn't there a better way to say it?"

"That is what happened," Joe said, and shrugged. "But we can call it a prank. I'm still not sure that's what it was, though." He wrote down *Prank?* under "What," then *Gym* under "Where."

"When—that's another easy one," Chet said. "This morning at around eight thirty a.m."

Frank was staring at the ceiling, studying the bucket that was still there, perched on one of the rafters. It looked like it was hooked up to some kind of electronic device, like it was automatic. "There's no strings or anything," he said. "Someone must have used a remote. They must've put it there before the assembly, maybe even before anyone came into school . . ."

"But why?" Joe asked. He tapped his pen on his notepad, looking at that word. "To ruin Chet's chances at becoming president? Or was it something more harmless? Did they just want to make a joke?"

"A joke!" Chet exclaimed. "Whoever did it must hate me. It was so embarrassing."

"Who wouldn't want you to win? Who would have a motive?" Frank asked. They used that word, "motive," a lot. It just meant why a person would want to do something. It was like describing someone's reason for stealing something, or playing a prank, or lying.

"There's the obvious answer," Joe said. He walked over to the first row and sat down. "Cissy wouldn't want Chet to win the election, because that would mean she'd lost for the first time ever at anything. But do you think Cissy would do something like that? Or Phil? He was helping her campaign, but still . . ."

Joe looked around at his friends. They all started laughing—even Chet. "No, definitely not," Chet said. "I don't think Cissy would do that."

"She's so honest!" Frank laughed. "Remember that time she found a hundred-dollar bill at the school carnival? She went around to everyone until she found out it belonged to Phil's grandfather. She could've just kept it, but she would never."

"Besides," Chet said, "Cissy's one of my good friends. Phil, too. I don't think they'd ever do that to me."

"I don't think so either," Joe said. He didn't even bother writing Cissy's or Phil's name down on the list. He wrote *Didn't want Chet to win* under "Why," but then he also wrote *Prank*. "Is there anyone you don't get along with? Anyone you can think of who would do that?"

Chet shrugged. "Not really."

"I don't know anyone who doesn't like you," Frank said. It was true. Chet was one of the friend-liest guys at school. Everyone was always saying how nice and funny he was. That was one of the reasons Frank and Joe had wanted him to run for class president in the first place. They knew he had a real chance.

Chet picked some of the dried slime from the back of his hair. "Well . . . ," he said, thinking. "Maybe there's one person."

"Who?" Joe asked. He brought his pen up, get-ting ready to write.

Chet sat down on one of the folding chairs beside Joe. "Rubin."

"Rubin Kratz?" Frank asked. Rubin was one of the biggest kids in the fourth-grade class. Everyone said he was going to grow up to be a really good athlete.

"Yeah, he's my lab partner," Chet said. "Something I did must've annoyed him. He kept making fun of me for running for president."

"Did you see him at the assembly?" Frank asked.

"No," Chet said. "I was looking for him, but he never showed up."

Joe wrote Rubin's name down under "Who" and smiled. Maybe it was only one suspect, but it was a start. "Let's go, then," he said, standing up. "I want to talk to Rubin."

5

On the Case

Chet stood but didn't follow them. He looked down at his stained shirt and pants. He had tucked the tie into his pocket, and the end of it was hanging out, still covered in green slime. "You guys should go," he said. "I can't go out there like this. I'll change into my gym clothes and try to wash the rest of this goo out of my hair."

He stared at his sneakers as he said it. Frank glanced sideways at his brother and frowned.

Chet had seemed better when they'd been asking him questions, but now he was upset again—it was obvious. "Don't worry," Frank said. "We'll find out who did this. Everything will be back to normal tomorrow, and you'll give one of the best speeches in Bayport history. No pranks and no slime."

"I hope," Chet said, before walking toward the locker rooms.

When the door shut behind him, Joe shook his head. "I feel so bad for Chet," he said. "He's really upset."

"I know," Frank said as he headed out the gym doors. They walked down the hall, past the cafeteria. Some kids were already going to their next class. A group of girls in front of them was laughing. Frank thought he overheard them whispering something about a prank, and slime, but he tried to ignore it.

"Do you really think Rubin would do something like that?" Joe asked. "He's kind of mean, but is he really mean enough to play a prank on Chet in front of the entire school?"

"I guess we'll find out," Frank said. He scanned the hallway, looking for any signs of Rubin. He was hard to miss. He was at least a foot taller than everyone else.

As they walked past the principal's office, Dr. Green peeked her head out of the door. "Frank! Joe!" she called. "Any luck so far?"

"Not yet," Joe said. "But we have a few leads."

Leads were the different people or places that the boys were going to investigate. Leads weren't as official as clues, but they were always a good place to start. Chet had given them the lead about Rubin, and now they would follow it and see what happened.

Dr. Green rubbed her hand across her forehead. "I wish I had more to tell you," she said. "I just held a teachers' meeting, but nobody saw anything strange. Whoever set up the prank must have done it early this morning, or maybe even yesterday when no one was looking."

Frank was about to tell her about the bucket, and how he thought the person must've used a remote, but just then a tall blond boy walked past. "Is that . . . ," Frank started.

"Rubin," Joe whispered. He grabbed his brother's arm and pulled him down the hall. "We have to go, Dr. Green!" he called out. "We might have something! But we gotta run!"

They didn't wait to hear Dr. Green's reply. A group of second graders was going out for recess and the halls were crowded now. The Hardys could see Rubin twenty feet ahead of them. He was walking alone through the fifth-grade wing.

The boys stayed close behind Rubin as he got to the end of the hall. Just when he was about to go down the stairs, Joe called out to him, "Hey, Rubin! Can we talk to you?"

Rubin turned around, looking at Frank and Joe, his blue eyes wide. They had never seen him seem scared before now. Rubin stood at the edge of the stairs for a moment, and then,

without saying a word, he ran down them.

"What was that about?" Frank asked. "Why would he run away like that?"

"He must be hiding something," Joe said.

They didn't wait another second. They took off toward the end of the hall, running after him.

6

The One That Got Away

By the time they got downstairs to the music wing, Rubin was already gone. There was a group of students waiting outside the band room, their instrument cases in their hands.

"Where did he go?" Frank asked, looking down to the end of the hall.

"It's like he disappeared," Joe said. He walked over to a boy with braces and freckles. The boy was holding a saxophone case. "Did you see a tall kid run past? Blond hair?"

"Yeah. He went down there," the boy said, pointing to a room two doors away. "The orchestra room, I think."

Frank and Joe thanked the boy, went two doors down, and opened the door just a crack. There were about fifty chairs set up with music stands. All of them were empty. Rubin wasn't there.

Joe put his finger over his lips as a

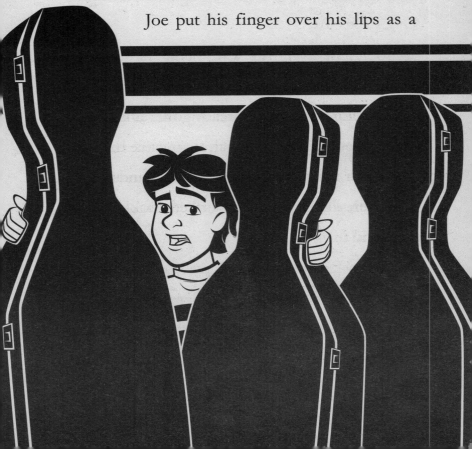

signal to Frank to be quiet as they snuck inside. Why was Rubin hiding from them? It seemed like proof that he'd done something wrong. Most students at Bayport knew that Frank and Joe were detectives who had solved many cases before.

"You go that way," Joe whispered, pointing to the side of the classroom with two pianos. "I'll check the closet."

Joe crept along the wall, being as quiet as he could. He'd been in the orchestra room only a few times before, mostly to visit his friend Callie. She sometimes liked to use lunch to practice her violin. He knew everyone kept their instruments in the closet. It seemed like the perfect place for someone to hide.

When he got to the closet door, he threw it open, turning on the light. There was a long row of black cases of all shapes and sizes. Rubin wasn't there. Joe was just about to turn around when he saw something move in the back corner. It looked like one of the cellos was swaying side to side.

"Rubin, I can see you!" Joe called. He turned back, waving for Frank to come over. "We know about the assembly today," Joe went on.

Rubin peered out from behind the giant cello case. "Please don't tell Dr. Green," he pleaded. "I already have three detentions. My dad's gonna be so mad at me."

Frank ran up behind Joe and stared into the narrow room. Rubin looked like he might cry at any moment. He sat against the wall and held his head in his hands. Normally Frank would feel bad for him, but he couldn't stop thinking about what Rubin had done to Chet. Chet didn't deserve to be made fun of like that or have his speech ruined.

"Dr. Green asked us to find out who did it," Frank explained. "We have to tell her. Besides, Chet is one of our best friends. Why would you play a prank on him in front of the whole school? Were you trying to ruin his campaign?"

Rubin looked up, his brows drawing together. "What are you talking about?"

"The bucket you put above the stage," Joe said. "As soon as Chet went up there to give his speech, you poured the slime down on him."

Rubin shook his head. "The slime? I wasn't even at the assembly this morning!"

Frank was confused. "Then what are you talking about?"

"I thought you knew that I skipped the assembly. I thought that was what you were talking about. I hate school elections. They're stupid," Rubin said.

"If you weren't in the gym this morning, then where were you?" Joe asked.

"I was outside, behind the playground. Adam and I play cards there sometimes. That game—Spit."

Frank knew the game. He and Joe played it

sometimes, usually when they went camping and they had only a deck of cards to keep busy with. "So you don't even know about the prank?"

Rubin shrugged. "What prank? I really don't have a clue what you're talking about."

Just then Frank heard a noise behind them.

"Rubin, you in here?"

Adam Ackerman came into the orchestra room. He was one of the biggest bullies in Bayport. He was always trying to get someone to give him their seat on the bus, or making one of the third graders buy him ice cream at lunch.

Rubin peered out of the closet door and waved at Adam. "Yeah, I'm here," he said. "I was just leaving, though."

"Are these dweebs bothering you?" Adam asked. He narrowed his eyes at Frank and Joe.

Frank ignored him. He'd known Adam since kindergarten—he was used to Adam calling them

names. "Were you at the assembly this morning?"
Frank asked Adam.

"Uh . . ." Adam looked behind Frank, at Rubin.

"Just tell them the truth. It's okay," Rubin said.
"They don't care if we skipped it. They're trying to
find out something about a prank."

Adam sighed. "We were out behind the playground, playing a card game. I beat Rubin for the third time this week."

Joe nodded, knowing what that meant. Rubin had an alibi, proof that he was somewhere else when the prank happened. There was no way he could've set off the bucket from all the way on the other

side of the school, outside, and behind the play-ground. It didn't matter if he liked Chet or not. He wasn't their suspect.

"Thanks, guys," Frank said as he headed toward the door. "We can check this off our list."

Joe followed behind him. When they were almost outside, Rubin called out to them. "Wait—you promise you won't tell on us?"

Frank shook his head. "Don't worry about it," he said. "That's not what we're interested in."

They slipped out the door and started down the hall. They should've felt better about what had just happened. They'd been able to cross Rubin off their list of suspects. The problem was that there had been only one person on that list . . . and now there were none.

"What are we going to do now?" Joe asked as they climbed the stairs. "If Rubin didn't do it, then who did?"

 **7**

The Evidence

Frank and Joe stood at the back of the gym, looking at the bucket above the stage. They'd decided to do what they always did when an investigation seemed to hit a dead end. . . . They'd gone back to the scene to take a second look.

"There has to be something we missed," Frank said, scanning the stage. He wasn't sure what he was looking for exactly, but he hoped there was some sort of clue the "slimer" had left behind. In their other cases suspects always left something behind!

The room was empty except for the janitor, Mr. Miles, who was folding up the chairs one by one. There was a ladder on the stage, just below where the bucket was still resting.

Frank and Joe walked down the aisle and checked behind the podium, where Chet had stood. The slime had been mopped up, and the microphone had been wiped clean. Frank crawled under the stage, but there was nothing there either.

"Mr. Miles?" Joe said, turning to the white-haired man behind them. "Do you think we can get that bucket down? We're looking for clues."

Frank went to climb the ladder, but Mr. Miles waved him away. "Let me get it for you—that's too high for you to climb up."

Mr. Miles climbed all the way to the top

while Frank and Joe held the bottom of the ladder for him. When he came back down, he handed them the bucket. "There you go," he said. "It was sitting on one of the rafters. Has a motor in it. . . . See here?"

He pointed to the bottom of the bucket, which had a hole in it. There was a thick plastic trapdoor. "You were right, Frank," Joe said. "Someone must've had a

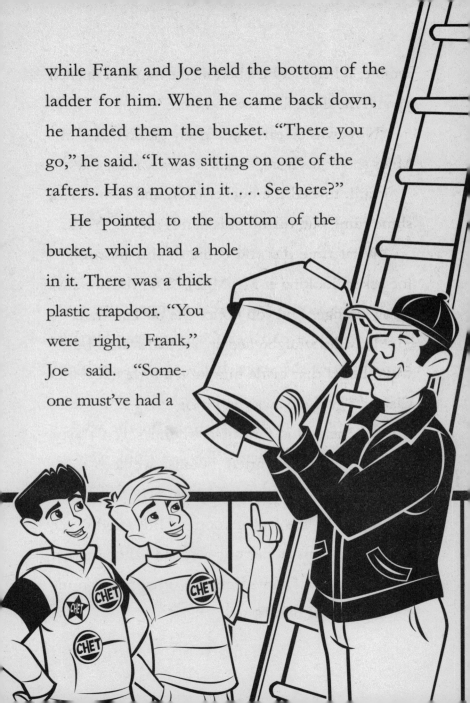

remote. When they hit a button, the trapdoor opened up and the slime fell down on Chet."

"Now, why on earth would anyone do that?" Mr. Miles shook his head. "Kids are crazy these days."

Frank turned the bucket over, and some extra slime came out, turning his hands green. "Yuck."

"What time did you come in this morning?" Joe asked, looking at Mr. Miles. "Did you see anything strange? Did you notice the bucket there?"

Mr. Miles straightened up. He had a large, bushy white beard that made him look a little like Santa Claus. "I get here every morning at six a.m. I went through here this morning around seven thirty, just before school started, because we keep some brooms in that closet over there." He pointed to the corner by the locker rooms. "But I didn't see the bucket. This ladder was out, and I thought that was strange. But sometimes the other guys on my staff move it. I don't know."

"So the ladder was out? By the stage?" Frank asked.

Mr. Miles pointed to the corner. "It was folded up over there. But it's normally in the closet."

"Did you notice anyone here who wasn't supposed to be? Any kids who came in early?"

Mr. Miles shook his head. "Nothing odd . . . no one I can remember. But now that you mention it, I did see something weird just before you got here, when I was cleaning up that mess."

He walked over to the garbage can in the corner and pointed into it. "What do you suppose those are?" he asked. "They looked strange to me. Might be connected to your prank."

Frank and Joe leaned closer. There wasn't much in the trash can except a couple of plastic jars on the bottom. The insides were coated with green slime. Frank reached in and plucked one out, studying it.

"Gross," Joe said, scrunching his nose up. "That had to have been what fell on Chet."

Frank flipped the plastic jar over. There was a small white tag on the bottom. "Look, a clue!" he said, squinting to read it. "Three dollars and ninety-nine cents. Crazy Eddie's."

"Crazy Eddie's?" Mr. Miles asked. "Isn't that the joke shop off Main Street?"

Joe smiled. "Yup, that's it. I went there last year for April Fools' Day to buy candies that turn your mouth blue."

"Whoever did this," Frank said, "they went to Crazy Eddie's to get the slime. Probably the bucket, too."

"We'll have to go there after school and see if anyone there knows anything," Joe said. "Maybe someone saw the person buy the slime."

"Thanks, Mr. Miles!" Frank said. "You gave us our first official clue. Without this, I don't know what we would've done."

Mr. Miles smiled down at the boys. "I'm just glad I could help. I'd hate to think whoever played this prank would get away with it."

"Hopefully, they won't!" Frank called over his shoulder as he waved good-bye to Mr. Miles.

Frank and Joe took the jar and started out the doors, more excited than ever. They knew where their suspect had been. Maybe, with a little luck, they could find out more about him.

 **8**

Crazy Eddie's: Gags, Gifts, and More!

That afternoon Frank and Joe's dad dropped them off outside Crazy Eddie's joke shop. The place was bright green on the outside with a yellow front door. Even the front window was full of things to play pranks with. There were whoopee cushions, squirting flowers, and fake piles of dog poop.

"I forgot how awesome this place is," Joe said

as they stepped inside. "Look! This is where I got that candy last year!"

The boys turned down an aisle with all different kinds of fake foods. There were ice cubes with flies and ants in them. They were perfect for putting in drinks to freak people out. There were candies like the one Joe had bought, that turned your mouth different colors. Frank grabbed a can of nuts and opened it. A giant snake popped out.

"Yikes!" he yelled, jumping back. "I didn't expect that."

Joe walked down the row, looking at bacon-flavored mints and bacon-smelling air freshener. Right next to those was a display of plastic sunny-side-up eggs you could put on the floor to fool people. "I could stay here all day," he said, picking up a package of rubber chocolates.

"We should find someone who works here," Frank said. He'd brought the plastic jar with him just in case. The label read FAKE SLIME in giant green letters.

They turned down another row, this one with different costumes. There were chicken and horse heads. There was a bunny suit and another costume that looked like a giant panda. At the end of it stood a man with orange hair. He was showing a woman a statue of a lion.

"Isn't this a nice statue?" he said, holding it up. It looked like it was made of gold. "Do you like it?"

The woman leaned closer. Right when her face was an inch away from it, water squirted out of the lion's mouth. The woman did not look happy. She mumbled something about manners before walking off in a huff.

"What can I help you boys with? Are you ready to get crazy at Crazy Eddie's?" The man's orange hair stuck up in different directions. He was wearing a rainbow-print bow tie and a nametag that said EDDIE. He leaned down, pointing the lion at Joe, but Joe ducked before Eddie could spray him with water.

Frank held up the empty jar. "Do you sell fake slime here?"

Eddie laughed. "Do we sell fake slime here? What kind of question is that?" He turned, waving for the boys to follow him. They went down another row filled with jars. "We got green slime, we got red slime, we got blue-and-purple-swirly slime. We got slime with eyeballs in it," Eddie said, pointing to the top shelf. "We got slime with fake brains in

it. You want bloody slime? We got that too!"

He held up a jar that looked like it was filled with blood and guts. There were fake fingers floating inside. "Ew!" Joe yelled. He took a step back, trying to get away.

"All I'm saying," Eddie continued, "is that we definitely have slime."

Frank scanned the shelves, and finally found the same container as the empty one they'd found at school. "Someone bought a few jars of fake green slime here," he said. "And maybe a bucket? With a remote?"

Eddie scratched the back of his head. "That sounds familiar." He peeked down the row and looked at the cashier, a teenage boy. "Hey, Gary! Do you remember someone coming in to buy green slime?"

"Yeah," Gary said, stepping out from behind the counter. "Like three days ago. You remember—he was asking you all about the remote control bucket. He bought that, too."

"That must be him!" Joe exclaimed. "He would've bought both of those things."

Gary ducked down another aisle and came back with the same kind of blue bucket that Frank and Joe had seen above the stage. This one had a remote with it. "See?" Gary asked. "Isn't it cool?"

He held the bucket up in the air, then hit a button on the remote. Tiny pieces of colored paper fell out of the bottom of the bucket. Frank grabbed a handful of it. "So it was a boy, then? How old?" Frank asked.

"Like your age, I guess." Gary shrugged. "He was a short kid, had a weird T-shirt on for some band."

Eddie shook his head. "Nope! I remember him—I know who you're talking about. He was tall. Had a blue T-shirt on—"

"I think it was green," Gary argued.

Frank snuck a quick look at his brother. This sometimes happened when they questioned witnesses. Everyone remembered things differently. The trick was finding what they both agreed on. "Did he have glasses? What color was his hair?"

"He definitely had glasses," Gary said.

But Eddie just shrugged. "You know, I don't think he did. But he had black hair."

"He's right about that," Gary agreed. "He had black hair."

Frank leaned in toward his brother. "That describes a ton of kids at Bayport. Black hair? That's all we have to go on?"

"What else?" Joe asked, trying to get at least a little more information out of them.

"He had a weird voice," Eddie said. "He talked like he was yelling."

Gary nodded his head. "Yeah, the dude sounded kind of loud."

Frank and Joe stayed in the joke shop, asking Eddie and Gary more about what the boy looked like, but they kept getting the same answers. There were no security cameras in the store, so there weren't any photos to check. After a few minutes they left and sat on the sidewalk, waiting for their dad to come back and pick them up.

"So he has black hair," Joe said, rubbing his chin with his hand. "And he talks like he's yelling. That isn't much help."

But Frank didn't respond. He was staring across the street, like he was thinking about something. "It might help . . . just enough."

"What do you mean?" Joe asked.

"Tomorrow," Frank said. "Let's go into school early, before anyone else. I think I have an idea."

9

Just a Hunch

Wait here with me," Frank said, standing against the wall by Dr. Green's office. "Just play along."

"Play along?" Joe asked. "Play along with what? Will you tell me what's going on already?"

"I did tell you," Frank said. "It's just a hunch . . ."

Normally Frank told Joe everything when they worked on a case together, but this time was different. Frank had said he had a "hunch" about something, and he wanted to follow it. A hunch was when someone had a feeling about something that they couldn't prove. He wasn't sure if he was right, so he didn't want to tell Joe about it just yet. Hopefully, Joe would make his own decision. Then they'd know if it was a lead to follow.

They'd gotten to school a half hour early and were standing in the hall as most of the students came in. After everyone was settled, the morning announcements were playing over the loudspeaker: "Because the assembly was cut short yesterday, all students should report to the gymnasium after these announcements. Both candidates will give their speeches for class president. Voting in the fourth-grade class election has been rescheduled and will go on this afternoon."

As the announcements went on, Chet walked past. He was wearing almost the same outfit as he'd worn the day before, but with a brand-new shirt and tie. He looked nervous. "I don't think I can do it," he said. "I can't go out there again. What if the same person decides to play a prank again? Maybe I should give up. Maybe we should just let Cissy win."

"Don't say that!" Joe cried. "Bayport Elementary fourth-grade needs you!"

Frank patted his friend on the shoulder. "We're going to figure this out. We'll meet you outside the gym in ten minutes. I think we're close."

"I hope so," Chet said. He pulled the speech from his pocket and started reading it to himself as he walked down the hall.

As soon as the morning announcements were over, the halls were crowded again. A group of fourth-grade boys pushed each other and laughed as they went toward the gym for the assembly. Frank watched the door to the main office. Eventually Art Carson came out. He'd just finished the announcements and started down the hall.

"Hey, Art!" Frank called. "I was hoping we could talk to you."

"Sure thing," Art said. "But can you walk with me to class?"

As soon as Art spoke, Joe knew what Frank's hunch was about. Art was always talking so loudly that he was nearly yelling. And he had spiky black hair and glasses. He might not have been who Eddie had described, but he fit Gary's description perfectly. Black hair. A band T-shirt. Glasses.

"We were just hoping you saw something yesterday," Frank said as the three boys continued down the hall. "You always get into school early, right? To do the announcements?"

"Yeah," Art said. "Dr. Green and I are the first ones here. I do the announcements from her office."

"Did you see anything strange?" Joe asked.

"Nah, I didn't even go past the gym yesterday." Art didn't look at them as he spoke. He just kept walking, picking up his pace. But it seemed like he was nervous. "I think I actually got in a little later than usual."

"When you went to the stage, did you notice the bucket above it? With the slime?" Frank asked.

"I—I don't remember," Art stammered.

"You don't remember?" Joe asked. He could tell Art was getting more and more nervous. Sometimes when the boys questioned suspects, the suspects got so nervous, they confessed. Would that happen now?

"Have you ever been to Crazy Eddie's?" Frank asked. "It's a joke store off Main Street."

Art's face turned red as soon as they mentioned the name of the store. "No, I've never gone there before," he said.

Frank felt like he might be closer to some answers. Why would Art get so upset because they mentioned the name of the store? Why was he bright red? Frank knew he had to keep questioning Art if he wanted to get these answers. "Really? You've never been in there?" he asked.

"I just told you, I have never bought anything from there," Art repeated.

"You haven't? Are you positive? It's a green store with a yellow door. It's hard to miss," Joe continued.

Art kept walking faster, then stopped outside the gym. "Fine!" he yelled. "I've been there. What's your point? Why do you care?"

"Were you there about three days ago buying green slime and a remote control bucket?" Frank asked.

"No . . . ," Art said, but his voice trailed off. "I just . . . Why are you asking me all of these questions?"

Just then Dr. Green walked up to them. "How are things going, Frank? Joe? Do you have any good news for me?"

"I think Art might have something to say," Frank said, nodding to Art.

"Who, me?" Art cried.

"The store clerk at Crazy Eddie's described you exactly," Frank said. "He said you were in there three days ago."

Dr. Green put her hands on her hips and frowned at Art. "Is this true? What are they talking about?"

Art took a deep breath. His face was bright red. "Okay! I did it!" he said, his voice cracking. "I didn't want Chet to win. I overheard you guys the other day, when Chet was practicing his speech. He said he wanted to give everyone a chance to do the morning announcements. The morning announcements are *my* thing!"

Dr. Green put her hands up in the air. "Are you saying you played that prank on Chet to ruin his speech and keep your spot?"

"I just didn't want him to win the election," Art repeated. "If *everyone* had the chance to read the announcements, they wouldn't be special anymore."

"So you bought the bucket and slime, then came in early to set up the prank . . . ," Frank said, talking it through.

"I used a ladder to put the bucket up there, right in the rafters above the stage. Then, when Chet started his speech, I hit the button on the remote," Art said. "I know it wasn't right, but it stopped the speech, didn't it? He couldn't finish."

Dr. Green just shook her head. "I'm so disappointed with you, Art," she said softly. "What you did yesterday was mean. Chet was so upset. You are one of our best students. How could you let me down like this?"

Frank watched Art, how his eyes filled with tears. Frank actually felt a little bad that they'd caught him, even if it was the right thing to do. Art seemed more upset than anyone else. Well, except Chet, of course. "I just . . . I'm sorry," he mumbled.

"Well, you're going to have to apologize to Chet now, in front of everyone," Dr. Green said. She waved him inside. "And no more announcements for you for the next two weeks."

"But, Dr. Green—"

"Don't argue with me, Art!" she said firmly. "Now go sit down inside. Wait for me to call you up."

Art stomped into the gym and sat down in one of the front seats. He crossed his arms over his chest. "He's so upset," Joe said, watching him.

"He should be upset," Dr. Green said. "What he did was wrong. And mean. Thank you for finding out who did this."

Joe and Frank stood in the gym doorway. Dr. Green went in, sat down beside Art, and whispered something to him. Even though he was the same age as Frank, he seemed so much younger now.

"Your hunch was right," Joe said.

Frank shrugged. "It seemed like Gary remembered the boy better than Eddie did. The description he gave was much clearer. Then, when I thought about who would be in school early enough to set up the prank, Art seemed like a suspect. I didn't realize he'd heard Chet giving his speech, though."

"Me neither," Joe said. "But it all makes sense."

The gym was nearly packed, with the fourth graders in the front few rows. All the seats were full except for a few in the back. This morning no one had signs. Only a few kids had remembered to wear their buttons. Most people weren't laughing or cheering. They were too afraid they'd get yelled at.

"We should go," Frank said, pointing to the locker room. "There's one person who will be very happy to hear the news."

10

The Race Is On

As soon as Frank and Joe walked into the locker room, they could hear Chet practicing his speech. He was somewhere near the back lockers. "Good morning, Bayport—I mean, good morning, students of Bayport—"

"Chet!" Joe called, turning the corner.

Chet was watching himself in the mirror on the wall. He held his speech out in front of him. "I don't think I can do this," he said. "I can't go out there again."

"But we found the person who played the prank—it was Art Carson," Joe said.

"He heard you practicing," Frank explained. "He was scared if you won that he wouldn't be able to read the morning announcements anymore. Dr. Green is going to have him apologize to you now, in front of everyone."

"You guys solved the case. That's amazing. I'm lucky to have friends like you," Chet said. He gave the boys a small smile.

"What's wrong?" Frank asked. Chet still seemed worried.

"It's just . . . ," Chet started. "I don't know. What if the prank ruined my chances of winning? What if people laugh at me? Someone yesterday called me slimeball in the hallway. I was so embarrassed."

"We'll be right there," Joe said, gesturing in the direction of the auditorium. "Right in the front row. If you get nervous, you can look at us. Pretend like it's just us there."

Frank jumped up onto one of the benches and smiled. "It's time for us to give you a little pep talk," he said. "Chet Morton, we know you can go out there and win today, no matter what happened yesterday. We became your campaign managers because we knew that Bayport Elementary needed a new fourth-grade president and that you were it. No one is as funny, as nice, or as smart as Chet Morton. And whenever you decide to do something, you really do it one hundred percent!"

"Yeah!" Joe said, raising his fist in the air. "You'll be the change this school needs."

That made Chet smile, at least a little bit. "You guys are really good friends."

"Are you ready?" Frank asked, jumping off the bench. He put his arm around Chet as they walked toward the locker room doors. Joe opened the door to the crowded gym just as Dr. Green was stepping onto the stage.

"I'd like to introduce our first candidate," she said. "Please give a round of applause for Chet Morton!"

Chet froze in the doorway. Everyone turned, watching him.

"You can do this," Joe whispered. "Look at those kids with BET ON CHET! buttons. Everyone is rooting for you. And remember—we'll be right in the front row if you need us."

Chet took one step forward, then another, slowly making his way toward the stage. Joe and Frank snuck into two open seats in the front row. When Chet got to the microphone, he took a few deep breaths, then began his speech.

"Good morning, students of Bayport Elementary. Most of you know me, and those of you who don't know me probably remember yesterday. . . . I know I do!" Chet smiled wide.

A few kids in the front row laughed. "But don't think I'm some *slimy* politician," Chet went on. "Or that I'll be *slippery* if things go wrong when I'm president."

As soon as the crowd realized he was kidding, more and more kids started laughing at Chet's jokes. Penny Cross, a girl with blond pigtails, nearly

spit when he made a joke about being "green" with envy of Cissy Zermeño's presidency.

As the speech went on, Chet became much more relaxed. He kept making different jokes to make the kids laugh. Then he went on to tell them what he'd do if he were fourth-grade class president. And besides things he wanted to do for his grade, he even talked about ideas for the school, too—like different lunch foods and his idea about morning announcements.

When he finished, the entire audience stood up and clapped. Even Cissy was cheering from where she was in the audience. "That was so brave of him to get back up there," a girl beside Joe said. "I can't believe he did it. I thought for sure he would drop out of the race."

Frank and Joe clapped so hard, their hands hurt. After Chet sat down beside them, they barely heard Cissy's speech or even the last few minutes of the assembly, when Dr. Green had Art get up and say sorry to Chet for what he'd done. They were too happy to notice any of it. They were just so proud of their friend.

"Everyone's saying they voted for you," Frank said as he sat down on the desk beside Chet. It was the last class of the day, social studies, and the winner of the fourth-grade election was going to be announced any minute. Mr. Parkins, their teacher, had let them take a break to talk.

"I don't know," Chet said. "People love Cissy. It's probably going to be pretty close."

"But so many kids I talked to loved your speech and said they would vote for you," Frank said. "Seriously. Almost every single one!"

It was true. People had been going up to Chet all day long and telling him how brave he was to do the speech again after what had happened yesterday. Some people were still laughing at his jokes. *He called himself a slimeball!* a girl in band had repeated. *That's so funny!*

That afternoon during lunch, everyone had gone to the cafeteria and used the voting booth one by one. Each student had a ballot to fill out and drop into the secret box inside the booth. For the last two hours Dr. Green and some of the teachers had been counting the ballots up to see who'd won. Any minute now they'd tell the whole school.

"I'm rooting for you, Chet!" a boy across the room called. He held up his button.

"Me too!" a girl said.

Cissy was in the class next door, but she'd stopped by before social studies to wish Chet luck. "Whatever happens," Chet said, turning to Frank, "I'm lucky to have you and Joe as friends."

Just then the loudspeaker on the wall crackled. Art normally did all the announcements, but instead it was Dr. *Green's voice that filled the* room. "Good afternoon, students of Bayport Elementary. Thank you all for voting today for your two candidates for fourth-grade class president. It was a very close race. I'm pleased to announce the next fourth-grade class president is . . ."

There was a long pause. Chet squeezed his eyes shut, scared of what she would say. "Chet Morton!" Dr. Green continued. "Congratulations, Chet! And thank you to Cissy Zermeño, who was a great leader this past year."

Chet stood up, and it seemed like the whole class rushed in around him. "You did it!" Frank cried. "You won!"

Chet threw his arms around his friends and hugged them as the rest of the class went wild. Some kids were cheering. Others were chanting "Bet on Chet!" Mr. Parkins had to tell one boy to not stand on his desk.

"No, Frank," Chet said, smiling bigger than ever. "*We* did it! *We* won!"

Frank and Chet high-fived. Frank couldn't wait to celebrate with Chet and Joe later. Their friend had gotten the votes he needed, and they'd been able to figure out who had played the prank on him. This case was officially closed.

SECRET FILES CASE #19: SOLVED!

FRANK AND JOE ARE VOLUNTEERING FOR THE BAYPORT ELECTION.

Now, boys, you wear these stickers and help anyone who needs it. I'll be checking people in.

It's official!

Now we just have to find something to do. It looks like everything is fine here. . . .

How much longer do we have to wait?! I can't just stand here all day!

Eeek! What are we going to do?! We don't know the answer to that.

But we don't need an answer. . . .

Excuse me, you! Young man! Can you help this gentleman? I have to warm up this bottle in the microwave.

Yup, be right back!